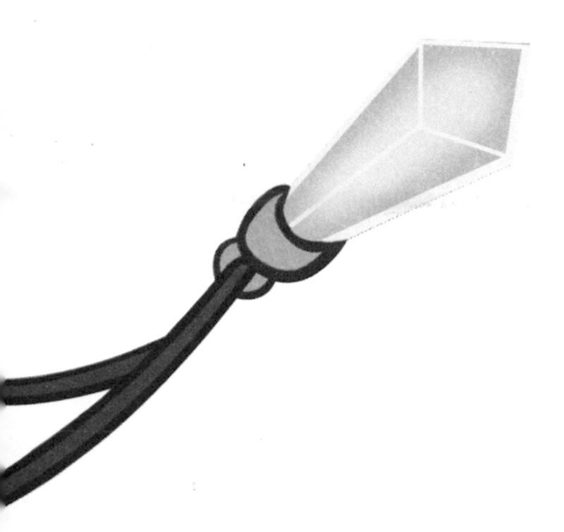

A NOTE TO PARENTS

When your children are ready to "step into reading," giving them the right books is as crucial as giving them the right food to eat. **Step into Reading Books** present exciting stories and information reinforced with lively, colorful illustrations that make learning to read fun, satisfying, and worthwhile. They are priced so that acquiring an entire library of them is affordable. And they are beginning readers with a difference—they're written on five levels.

Early Step into Reading Books are designed for brand-new readers, with large type and only one or two lines of very simple text per page. **Step 1 Books** feature the same easy-to-read type as the Early Step into Reading Books, but with more words per page. **Step 2 Books** are both longer and slightly more difficult, while **Step 3 Books** introduce readers to paragraphs and fully developed plot lines. **Step 4 Books** offer exciting nonfiction for the increasingly independent reader.

The grade levels assigned to the five steps—preschool through kindergarten for the Early Books, preschool through grade 1 for Step 1, grades 1 through 3 for Step 2, grades 2 through 3 for Step 3, and grades 2 through 4 for Step 4—are intended only as guides. Some children move through all five steps very rapidly; others climb the steps over a period of several years. Either way, these books will help your child "step into reading" in style!

Published in the United States by Random House, Inc., New York, and simultaneously in Canada by Random House of Canada Limited, Toronto, in conjunction with Disney Enterprises, Inc.

Library of Congress Card Catalog Number: 00-110427

ISBN: 0-7364-1085-6

www.randomhouse.com/kids/disney
www.disneybooks.com

Printed in the United States of America May 2001

10 9 8 7 6 5 4 3 2 1

Step into Reading®

Disney's

ATLANTIS
THE LOST EMPIRE

KIDA AND THE CRYSTAL

By K. A. Alistir

Illustrated by the Disney Storybook Artists at Global Art Development, Denise Shimabukuro, and Samantha Clarke

Painted by John Raymond, Adam Devaney, Ken Becker, Brent Ford, and Todd Ford

Designed by Disney's Global Design Group

A Step 3 Book

Random House New York

Chapter 1:
The Great Flood

Far out in the Atlantic Ocean, a tidal wave was forming. It grew to a monstrous size, rolling straight for the city of Atlantis.

The people began to run for shelter. But it was hopeless. The wave was about to swallow their entire island in one giant gulp!

This can't be happening, the king of Atlantis told himself as the royal family raced for the palace. Atlantis was a powerful city. How could it be in danger?

The queen saw the fear in the king's eyes. "Come quickly, Kida!" she cried to their little girl. But Princess Kida lagged behind. She had dropped her favorite doll.

"Kida! Just leave it!" cried the queen.

Suddenly, a bright red light filled the sky. The light was coming from the giant crystal that floated above the city.

The light turned into a blue beam when it fell upon the queen. The beam pulled her up into the Crystal. Kida's hand slipped out of her mother's.

"Mama!" Kida cried. But the queen had already disappeared into the Crystal.

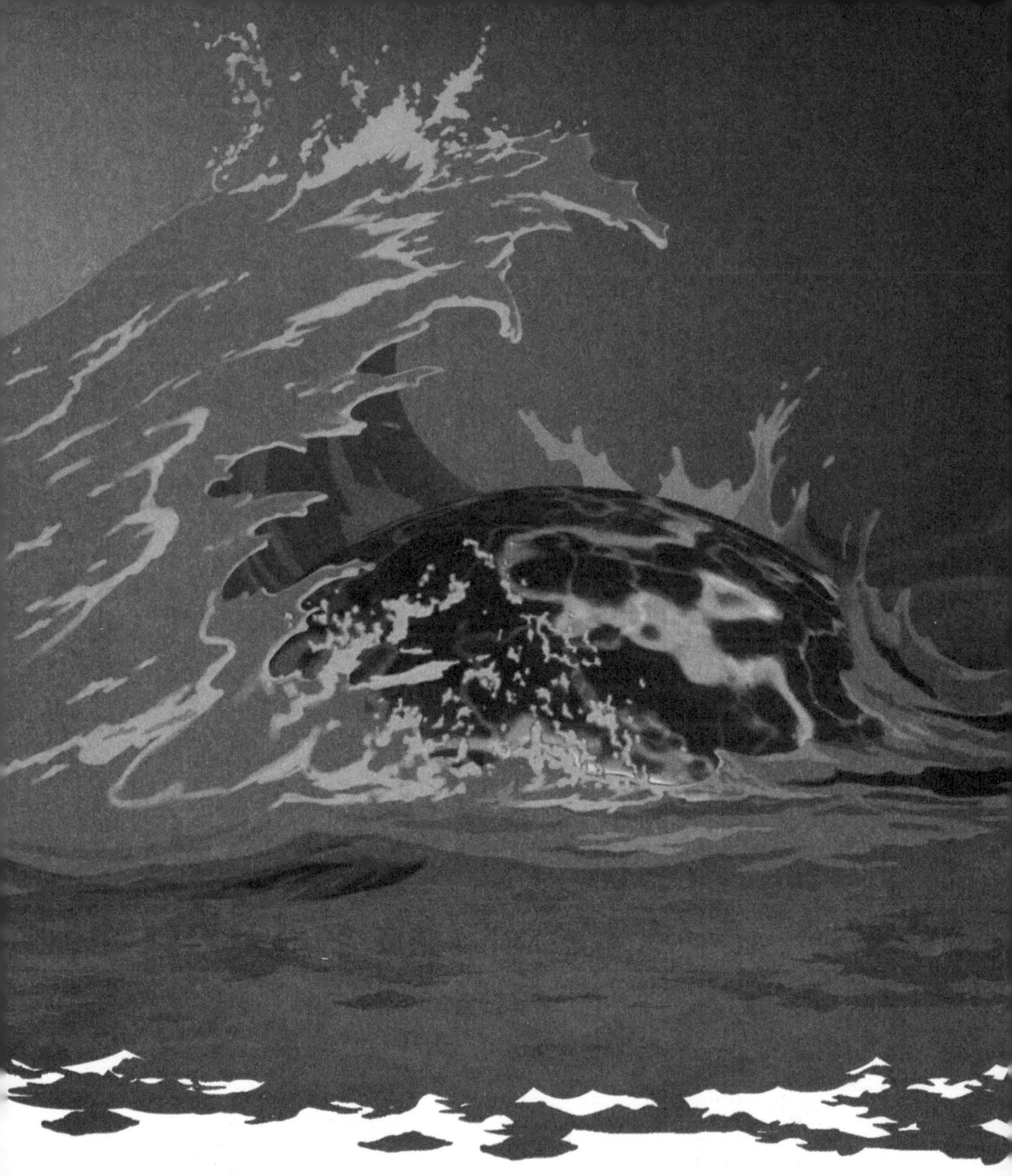

Moments later, more beams of blue light shot down from the Crystal. The light surrounded Atlantis like a protective bubble.

And then the tidal wave hit! It crashed against the bubble. But the city was safe.

The island of Atlantis began to sink. Down, down, down—deep into the blue ocean waters. Away from the rest of the world.

Atlantis and its people were saved. But it was no longer the greatest city in the world. It was now a lost empire, hidden deep below the earth's surface!

Chapter 2:
The King's Secret

Many years passed. Princess Kida grew into a beautiful young woman. She had long white hair and wide blue eyes.

"She looks just like her father," the people of Atlantis whispered. They thought Kida wasn't listening. But the princess was *always* listening—and learning.

She wanted to find out why Atlantis had sunk into the ocean. She wanted to learn more about an old memory—about the bright light that had lit up the sky. But mostly, she wanted to find out what had happened to her mother.

One day, Kida visited her father in his throne room.

"Father, tell me again about the Great Flood," she said.

The king did not like to talk about the past. "We cannot change our history," he told his daughter.

Kida jumped to her feet. "Maybe by learning about the past, we can help Atlantis grow strong again."

"Enough, Kida!" the king grumbled. He would not tell his daughter the secrets of Atlantis. Kida grabbed her hunting spear and ran down the palace steps. She was angry with the king. Lately, they could not agree on anything.

She decided to go exploring.

Chapter 3:
The Stranger from Above

"Let's prepare for the hunt!" Kida called to her warrior friends. She pulled her hunting mask over her head. Then the group set off.

“Take that! And that!” the princess shouted, practicing her favorite kicks. She leaped into the air. No one messed with Kida. She was an excellent hunter and warrior.

Kida and her friends explored a maze of caves, looking for cave beasts.

But they found something much more interesting.

The hunting party discovered a group of explorers from the surface world! Kida and her warriors followed them for a while. Then one of them became separated from the others. He was hurt!

Kida went to take a closer look. The young man was dressed in strange clothes. Slowly, he opened his eyes. His shoulder was bleeding. Kida took off her crystal necklace. She placed the crystal on the man's shoulder. In a flash, the wound was healed!

Then more people arrived. They were friends of the young man. "Welcome to the city of Atlantis," Kida told them. "Come, you must speak with my father."

The king was not happy to see the visitors. He wanted them to leave.

"But these people may be able to help us," Kida said. The king shook his head. He insisted that the visitors leave Atlantis the next day.

Chapter 4:
Questions and Answers

Kida was disappointed. She wanted answers to her questions.

She found one of the explorers waiting outside the throne room. He was the man she had healed. His name was Milo.

"I have some questions for you." Kida grabbed his arm. "And you are not leaving this city until they are answered!"

Milo agreed. He was just as curious about Atlantis as the princess was!

The princess led Milo to a cave. There she told him about the Great Flood.

"My father said the gods were jealous of Atlantis. They sank the city into the ocean." She told him about the bright light, and how her mother had disappeared.

"You were there?" Milo cried. "That would make you more than eight thousand years old!"

"Yes," Kida said.

"Hey! Looking good," Milo joked.

Next it was Milo's turn to share.

"How did you find this place?" Kida asked.

Milo showed the princess an ancient leather book—*The Shepherd's Journal.* It was filled with information about Atlantis. Milo said it was his dream to find out exactly what had happened to the city.

Kida's eyes shone. "It is my dream, too," she said softly.

The princess stared at the worn journal. Milo was surprised to learn she could not read.

"Since the Great Flood, no one has been able to read," Kida explained sadly. "Our history was lost."

Suddenly, she had an idea. She led Milo farther into the cave.

Under a thick cloth stood a fish-shaped vehicle. “This is a Ketak,” explained Kida.

“Wow! It looks like something you drive,” said Milo.

“Yes,” said Kida. “But I can’t make it work.”

Chapter 5:
The Flying Fish

Milo read the directions carved into the top of the Ketak to Kida. Following them, she placed her crystal in a slot. The vehicle started up and rose into the air!

“With this thing, I can see the whole city in no time!” Milo shouted above the noise of the engine.

Then Milo placed his hand on the Ketak.
Zap! It took off by itself.

Bang! The Ketak flew around in circles, bouncing against the walls.

Milo and Kida dove for cover. The Ketak stopped with a crash.

Maybe walking would be best, Milo thought.

Kida decided to take Milo on a tour of the city—on foot. They walked to an outdoor marketplace.

"Are you hungry?" asked Kida.

"I sure am," said Milo. Then he saw Kida approaching a booth that was selling long, gooey tentacles wrapped around a stick. "I sure am . . . not hungry anymore," he added quickly.

Kida paid the man at the booth. "Tastes good," she said, biting off a tentacle. She offered Milo a taste.

Milo took a small bite. "Mmmm . . . ," he said. "Not bad. But it could use some ketchup."

Chapter 6:
The Same but Different

Milo was just finishing one last tentacle when he saw a strange sight.

“Um, Kida,” he said, pointing toward a creature he had never seen before, “what is that?”

“That’s a shemubin, of course,” said Kida.

“Sheh-who-bin?” said Milo.

Kida explained that the friendly creature was a popular pet in Atlantis. She patted the shemubin. “Now you try it,” she told Milo.

“Hey, I want to keep that hand!” Milo cried as the creature slobbered all over him.

Next Milo and Kida played an Atlantean game. "You have to try to knock down the fish statues with this ball," explained Kida.

Crash! Slam! Milo knocked all the statues down.

“That was great!” said Kida.

“Well, I *am* the champ at my local Bowl ’n’ Burp Lanes,” said Milo.

Milo won a prize—another helping of tasty tentacles on a stick!

“Kida! Kida!” A little girl ran up to Kida and Milo.

“Hello, Tali.” Kida gave the girl a big hug.

“You’re coming to my birthday party, right?” asked Tali.

“Of course,” said Kida. “A girl doesn’t turn fifteen hundred every day.”

Milo had a fun time at the party.

"Um . . . Milo," said Kida, "you're using an Atlantean hairbrush to eat your cake."

The cake tasted even better when Milo ate it with an Atlantean fork.

Chapter 7:
The Story of Atlantis

Milo and Kida left the party and hiked to the top of a hill overlooking the city. Milo gazed down at Atlantis.

"The most my team hoped to find was some crumbling buildings," he told Kida. "Instead, we found a whole city full of people!"

But the princess just shook her head sadly. Her people were in trouble. The city was slowly falling apart. Every year it was harder to find food. Every year they forgot more of their history.

Kida brought Milo to a pool of water.

"I have brought you to this place to ask for your help," she told Milo. "Follow me."

Kida dove into the water. Milo followed close behind. Soon they were swimming past the flooded ruins of ancient Atlantean buildings. Colorful murals and Atlantean writing covered the walls. Milo could hardly believe his eyes. It was a painted history of Atlantis!

"This is amazing!" Milo said when they came up for air. "The history of Atlantis is painted on these walls!" Milo held up Kida's glowing crystal necklace.

Kida could barely speak. Milo could tell her the whole story!

At last she would learn about her people. And maybe she would discover what had happened to her mother.

"Does the writing say anything about the light I saw?" Kida asked Milo.

They took deep breaths and dove back under the water.

In one drawing, Milo saw a large crystal falling from the sky. In another drawing, people were wearing pieces of the Crystal around their necks.

Chapter 8:
The Heart of Atlantis

Milo and Kida swam up for air.

"The light that you saw," Milo explained to the princess, "is the Heart of Atlantis. It is a power source. It keeps everyone and everything in Atlantis alive."

Kida nodded slowly. She could guess why her father kept the Heart of Atlantis a secret. He feared that its great power would be misused.

Kida remembered the last time she had seen the huge crystal. Her mother had floated up into its blue light. The Crystal had taken the queen. As soon as she had disappeared, Atlantis had been saved from the tidal wave. The queen had given her life for the sake of the city!

Kida hugged Milo. “Thank you for your help,” she said.

Milo blushed. The princess smiled.

Not only had she found out the truth about Atlantis, she had also made a wonderful new friend!

As Milo swam back to the surface, Kida took another long look at the pictures on the wall. The pictures showed the history of her city—and told the story of her family.

"Thank you, Mother," she whispered, "for all you have done for us."

Just then, the crystal around Kida's neck began to glow. Kida knew it was a message from her mother. "Be brave," the crystal seemed to say. "Be strong."

And Kida *was*. With Milo's help, she was ready to unlock *all* the secrets of Atlantis.